S0-EAV-572

Behind The Wheel™

Jeff Gordon

NASCAR Driver

J. Poolos

rosen publishing's
rosen central®

New York

Published in 2007 by The Rosen Publishing Group, Inc.
29 East 21st Street, New York, NY 10010

Copyright © 2007 by The Rosen Publishing Group, Inc.

First Edition

All rights reserved. No part of this book may be reproduced in any form without permission in writing from the publisher, except by a reviewer.

Library of Congress Cataloging-in-Publication Data

Poolos, J.
Jeff Gordon: NASCAR driver / J. Poolos. — 1st ed.
    p. cm. — (Behind the wheel)
Includes bibliographical references and index.
ISBN-13: 978-1-4042-0980-0
ISBN-10: 1-4042-0980-8 (library binding)
1. Gordon, Jeff, 1971– —Juvenile literature. 2. Automobile racing drivers—United States—Biography—Juvenile literature.
I. Title.
GV1032.G67P66 2007
796.72092—dc22
[B]
                                        2006021394

Manufactured in the United States of America

On the cover: Jeff Gordon takes part in the MBNA Armed Forces Family 450 on June 1, 2003.

CONTENTS

CHAPTER 1

Back on Top

It had been a wild and woolly finish, but there he was again, standing in the winner's circle, pumping his fist in the air and shouting at the top of his lungs. A wide grin was spread across his face. Jeff Gordon had won the 2005 Daytona 500, the biggest stock-car race in the world. In winning his third career Daytona 500, Gordon had become only the fifth driver in the history of NASCAR to win three or more 500s at the famed Daytona raceway, joining such stock-car racing legends as Richard Petty, Cale Yarborough, and Bobby Allison. Though he had previously won four NASCAR championships, the last few years had seen the champ struggle to finish on top. And this victory was as sweet as any.

Rival driver Tony Stewart had utterly dominated the race, leading a total of 107 laps. But

Jeff Gordon celebrates victory in the NASCAR Nextel Cup Daytona 500 on February 20, 2005, at Daytona International Raceway, the biggest race of the year.

several crashes late in the going allowed other drivers to catch the leader, and with three laps to go, it was anyone's race. A struggling Dale Earnhardt Jr. had come from as far back as 30th place to take the lead, only to see Gordon pass him seconds before a crash slowed down the action.

As the cars paraded around the track at caution pace and cleanup crews gathered debris from the track, Gordon plotted his strategy. He knew the guys behind him wanted to win as much as he did. And he knew they would try to draft him onto the last straightaway before the finish line, or maybe even try to bump him out of the way. He would have to defend the inside all the way down to the apron.

On May 1, 2005, Gordon leads at the Aaron's 499 in Talladega, Alabama, in his #24 DuPont Chevrolet. This race became Gordon's third Aaron's 499 win.

When the green flag dropped to signal the end of the caution, the air filled with thunder as the cars roared off in pursuit of Gordon's #24 Chevrolet Monte Carlo. Kurt Busch, the defending NASCAR champion, stuffed his Ford past Earnhardt and bore down on Gordon. Behind the leaders, other cars were bumping one another in an effort to gain position. Gordon pushed as hard as he could and held off the charging Busch and Earnhardt to take the checkered flag.

The year before, Gordon had narrowly missed out on winning his fifth NASCAR championship, trailing winner Busch by 16 points and Hendrick Motorsports teammate Jimmie Johnson by 8. It had been three years since his last championship, plenty of time to wonder if it was his driving, his will to win, or maybe his car that was keeping him from victory. But all of that was behind Jeff Gordon as he stood in the winner's circle, shaking hands and slapping the backs of his crew. He was through with asking questions. It was time to race, and he was back on top.

First Steps

Jeffrey Michael Gordon began his journey to superstardom at an early age. Born August 4, 1971, in Vallejo, California, just 25 miles (40 kilometers) from San Francisco, Jeff learned to ride a bicycle when he was three years old. He began racing BMX a year later, at an age when most kids are still riding with training wheels. Soon he was racing against kids twice his age and pushing himself to the limit. His mother, Carol, his older sister, Kimberly, and his step-father, John Bickford, attended the races to support Jeff. One day, after witnessing one of Jeff's many crashes, Carol decided to put an end to his BMX racing. She suggested to

John that they find a safer activity for Jeff, and Bickford, a die-hard racing enthusiast, had a surprise in mind.

One day, not too long after Jeff's last BMX race, John came home with a pair of midget race cars, one for Jeff and one for his eight-year-old sister. They built a track near the local fairgrounds, and Jeff spent afternoons driving the tiny, 2.85-horsepower car faster and faster. Jeff's stepfather coached him along the way. After about a year, he decided it was time for Jeff to start racing.

A Champion Is Made

Jeff took part in local midget car races, and the young-ster showed promise. He soon began to run in races outside his region. Jeff practiced three days a week, every week of the year. At eight years old, he won his first national championship in the quarter midget class. Looking for a new challenge, Jeff moved up to the next fastest class, where he drove go-karts with 10-horse-power engines. The 9-year-old raced kids as old as 17 and beat them all. He quickly moved up to the next class and found himself racing guys in their late teens and early twenties. These racers didn't take kindly to such a young kid beating them to the finish line.

The next year John decided the boy should return to the quarter midgets so he could race against kids closer to his age. No one could touch him, and again Jeff won the national championship. John realized Jeff was something special as a driver. Jeff, too, felt like he had accomplished his goals racing the midget cars and wanted to take on a bigger challenge. The problem was that there were no opportunities for him to grow as a racer. Kids his age just weren't allowed to drive the big cars. So John started looking for racing opportunities outside of California. He found a circuit in the Midwest where there was no age limit, and the family moved to Indiana to pursue Jeff's racing career.

They settled in the town of Pittsboro, Indiana. Pittsboro was only 20 miles (32 km) from Indianapolis, where the biggest race in the United States, the Indianapolis 500, is run each year. John built Jeff a sprint car, a $25,000 machine with a 650-horsepower engine. The sprint car was quite a jump from the karts Jeff was used to driving. He started racing the Midwest sprint-car circuit, competing against the region's best up-and-coming drivers. He was only 13 years old.

The Move to Big Cars

After driving the winter circuit in Florida in 1985, Jeff tore onto the scene like a cyclone, racing on short oval tracks across Indiana, Illinois, and Ohio. The competition was fierce, and the drivers were much more experienced than he was. But Jeff showed a lot of promise for a kid who wasn't even old enough to have a driver's license. He won a few races, drove consistently, and learned a great deal about racing tactics.

NASCAR'S INAUSPICIOUS BEGINNINGS

Stock-car racing is a purely American creation. Its roots are in the South in the 1920s and early 1930s. This was the period of Prohibition, when the sale of alcoholic beverages was against the law. Homemade liquor, known as moonshine, was produced and sold illegally. Moonshine was delivered by drivers whose job was to outrun the police. Occasionally, one driver would challenge another to a backyard race. Eventually, these impromptu races led to more organized events, often promoted by shady individuals who tried to cash in on the races. These promoters were often dishonest and skipped out with the prize money before the races were finished.

One man sought to promote these races honestly. William "Big Bill" France, a mechanic and driver, took his interest in racing to Florida. He became a promoter of the first races on the beach at Daytona. In his second year as promoter, he sold 4,500 tickets at 50 cents each. France had no idea he was building the foundation of the NASCAR Winston Cup Series.

As more legitimate stock-car racing took hold in the East, France got the idea to hold a national championship. On December 12, 1947, he helped construct a set of rules and a sanctioning body. On February 21, 1948, NASCAR was born, with France as its president.

When he turned 18 years old, Jeff had to make some decisions about his life. Until that point, he had thought of racing merely as a fun thing to do. But it was time for him to decide how to make a living. He had built his identity around racing, as had his mother and stepfather. The option to become a professional racer was open to him, but he thought he might like to go to college and choose a more traditional career. It was the most serious decision he had faced thus far. In the end, he chose racing, and from then on he was a different person.

The Next Level

Jeff drove a variety of cars, including heavy sprint cars with 800-horsepower engines. He also won the 1991 United States Auto Club midgets championship that year. The next step up the ladder was stock-car racing.

Jeff got his first taste of a high-performance stock car while attending NASCAR legend Buck Baker's racing school. Shortly thereafter, he was entered in the Busch Grand National Series. This series was the feeding ground for NASCAR's Winston Cup division (now called the Nextel Cup). That year, Jeff was so dominant he won Rookie of the Year honors. The kid who, not long ago, was circling a dirt lot in a little car with a lawnmower engine clearly had a very promising future. He was one step from the most prestigious stock-car series in the world.

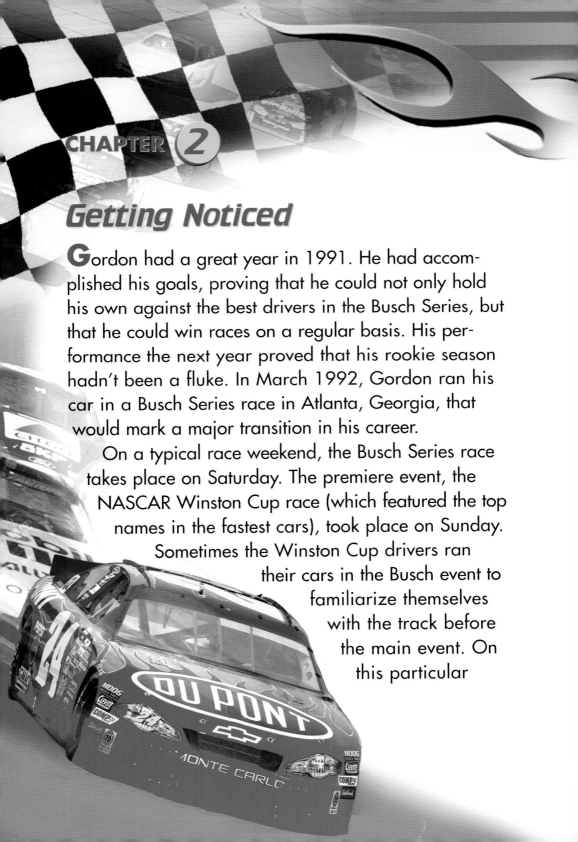

CHAPTER 2

Getting Noticed

Gordon had a great year in 1991. He had accomplished his goals, proving that he could not only hold his own against the best drivers in the Busch Series, but that he could win races on a regular basis. His performance the next year proved that his rookie season hadn't been a fluke. In March 1992, Gordon ran his car in a Busch Series race in Atlanta, Georgia, that would mark a major transition in his career.

On a typical race weekend, the Busch Series race takes place on Saturday. The premiere event, the NASCAR Winston Cup race (which featured the top names in the fastest cars), took place on Sunday. Sometimes the Winston Cup drivers ran their cars in the Busch event to familiarize themselves with the track before the main event. On this particular

At the 2006 Coca-Cola 600, Gordon speaks with team owner Hendrick. Gordon led for 18 of the 360 laps before crashing out of the race.

Saturday, some of the Winston Cup's finest took part in the Busch race, including perennial front-runner Dale Earnhardt. Gordon was trading paint with the best of them.

One of the sport's most influential players, Rick Hendrick, witnessed the youngster driving his car on the edge of control. Gordon swung his car into the corners, tires smoking, running so fast he could barely hold his racing line. At first, the experienced Hendrick, who owns a number of Winston Cup cars, thought Gordon was just another young gun driving beyond his limits in an effort to keep up with the more established drivers. He had seen them before. They drove fast for a number of laps but eventually pushed too hard and lost control, spinning out or crashing. In Hendrick's experience, only the best drivers could sustain that kind of pace. But Gordon kept on going, clinging to the tails of Earnhardt and the other leaders.

After the race, Hendrick sought out Gordon and was surprised at how mature he was for someone so young. Hendrick was so impressed that he signed Gordon to a contract. That year, Gordon went on to win a series record 11 pole positions and 3 Busch races. In the autumn race in Atlanta, Hendrick gave Gordon his big break when he entered him in the Winston Cup race— his first shot at the ultimate in stock-car racing.

Hendrick figured this was a chance to see what Gordon could do racing against the best. It was the last race of the season, and he wanted to give the youngster the chance to get his feet wet before the 1993 season, when he planned for Gordon to run the Winston Cup Series all year long. That race, Gordon qualified 21st and finished 31st. It was an unremarkable result, but he had followed team orders to run a conservative race and finish without crashing. In that sense, Gordon had accomplished his goals, and he had a taste of what it was like to race against the top drivers and the best cars.

Making a Mark

Having run a complete race in the Winston Cup Series the year before, Gordon started the 1993 season well aware of what he was in for: serious competition from the skilled drivers for which the series is famous. He had spent the off-season preparing for his rookie year, and when the first race weekend came around, he was ready.

The first race of the season is always the Daytona 500. One thing that set the Winston Cup apart from other sports series is the fact that while most sports series open the season with "regular" events and build up to more grand events, NASCAR opens the season with the year's biggest event. For several days prior to the event, teams run qualifiers, which are shorter races that lead up to the 500-mile (805 km) slugfest. They use these qualifiers to fine-tune their cars, practice their pit stops, and get back in the groove after the off-season.

Qualifiers also set the tone for the 500. Gordon stunned the field when he won one of the qualifying races, becoming the youngest driver in the history of the Daytona 500 to win a qualifier. Later that weekend, he would earn the respect of his fellow drivers by placing a very impressive fifth at the 500.

In 1993, there was a marked change in NASCAR, with an influx of quality rookie drivers, among them Bobby Labonte, who would become Winston Cup champion in 2000. Pundits predicted a tight competition between the two, as well as Kenny Wallace, for Rookie of the Year honors. But it wasn't even close. One of Gordon's preseason goals was to win the

Gordon holds the trophy for fifth place at the Daytona Speedway on February 14, 1993. Days before, the rookie stunned the crowd when he won a qualifying race for the 500.

award, and win it he did. While Labonte and Wallace struggled to come to terms with the fierce competition, Gordon placed in the top ten at 11 races.

There's More to Life Than Racing

The 1994 season was a dream come true. Besides winning two races, Gordon put together a string of consistent finishes only the best of the truly seasoned drivers could hope for. The winning season was made even sweeter by an important change in Gordon's personal life. At the start of the season, he made an announcement that stunned everyone: He was engaged to a woman named Brooke Sealy, who was Miss Winston during the 1993 season.

One of Miss Winston's responsibilities is to greet the winner of each race at the winner's circle, which is where

Gordon met Sealy after he won the Daytona qualifier at the beginning of 1993. Throughout the year, the two carried on a secret relationship because drivers were forbidden to socialize with Miss Winston. Yet Gordon uncharacteristically broke the rules and dated her anyway. When they wanted to spend time together, they had to do so away from their NASCAR friends. Sometimes they would have to attend NASCAR functions, such as dinners, ceremonies, and promotional events. Because they didn't want anyone to know they were dating, they behaved as if they didn't know each other.

Soon after the engagement, on November 26, 1994, Gordon and Sealy married amid great publicity. After a honeymoon in St. Martin, they moved into a home near Charlotte, North Carolina. Sealy's influence on Gordon was refreshingly positive. He attributed his focus and his success to her presence in his life.

Hometown Hero

Two months after Gordon's first victory, he traveled to Indianapolis to run the inaugural Brickyard 400. The Indianapolis Speedway is host to the country's most famous open-wheel car race, the Indianapolis 500, which draws crowds in excess of 250,000 from around the country. All of the drivers wanted to win this race and show the world that stock-car racing was serious business. But no one wanted to win it more than

Gordon and Sealy pause for a moment next to the #24 car during a break in the action at the Daytona Speedway in February, 1997.

Gordon. He had grown up just 15 miles (24 km) from the track, and he wanted nothing more than to win in front of his home crowd.

There was great anticipation for the event among the media as well, and the $3.2 million purse was the largest in NASCAR history. As the teams practiced over the few days leading up to the race, anticipation for a great race built. There was tension in the air, and Gordon was right in the thick of it. In the race itself, he didn't disappoint, running strong through the better part of the race. Gordon found himself locking horns with series points leader Ernie Irvan, and the two dueled for nearly 30 laps. First Irvan would lead, then Gordon would draft by

Gordon's #24 car screams across the finish line after a battle with Ernie Irvan at the inaugural Brickyard 400, held at Indianapolis Speedway, only a few miles from his hometown.

him to go out front. Finally, Gordon slotted his car right on Irvan's tail in an attempt to pressure the veteran into a mistake. At worst, he thought, he could try to pass Irvan one last time and cross the finish line for the win.

Gordon drove right up on Irvan's back bumper to try to "push" him off-line. This is a technique stock-car drivers use to take advantage of the effects of air turbulence on the lead car. By driving into a car's slipstream, a driver can disrupt the airflow over that car so that it's harder to control. The lead driver can't feel what the car is doing, and in the most successful cases, the lead car will lose some of its handling ability. In fact, sometimes this effect can cause the driver to lose so much rear-wheel

Gordon celebrates after winning the Brickyard 400. The race, which was run on the legendary Indy car track, paid a $3.2 million purse, at that time the largest in the history of NASCAR.

traction that he spins the car out, even without contact between the two cars.

Though Irvan held his ground and didn't make any mistakes, Gordon's pressure took its toll on his car. With only five laps to go, Gordon decided he would take another shot at the lead and swung his car alongside Irvan, outside of the racing groove. The two cars howled down the straightaway. But suddenly Gordon pulled away. Irvan's car had slowed down dramatically. His right front tire had a cut, and his race for victory was over. Gordon cruised home to take the checkered flag. He would go down in history as the victor of the first stock-car race ever staged at the Indianapolis Motor Speedway.

Everyone in NASCAR knew Gordon had potential to be a great driver. He had shown it when he won the qualifier at Daytona and when he won at Charlotte. At the Brickyard 400, when Gordon came down the pit lane after his victory lap, it seemed that even his competitors recognized that his moment had come. Guys from other pit crews waved and gave him the thumbs-up sign, and when he got out of his car, he was mobbed by his own crew. It was a great feeling. Not only had he driven a brilliant race, he had also given the hundreds of thousands of fans in the grandstands and the millions watching on television a truly great show.

A Championship Season

Gordon went on to have even more success that year, with 14 top-ten finishes and 7 top-fives in the 31-race season. But it was 1995 that would prove to be his banner year. He started the year strongly and looked to be a lock for the title. But reigning Winston Cup king Dale Earnhardt wasn't about to give up his throne.

Gordon's Hendrick Chevrolet ran well and he drove like a seasoned pro, but the team struggled as the season wore on. Earnhardt seized his chance, making a heroic run for the championship. With four races to go, the third-year driver led the defending champ by 302 points. But on lap 139 of the race, the Hendrick Chevy broke a driveshaft while exiting pit row. This was a nearly catastrophic failure. Dale Earnhardt came on strong to finish second

On October 29, 1995, at the Dura Lube 500 at Phoenix International Raceway in Arizona, Gordon held off a charging Dale Earnhardt to win his second Winston Cup NASCAR Championship.

to Mark Martin. Gordon finished 30th, his lead cut down to 205 points.

Earnhardt had just begun his assault on Gordon's massive points lead. With three races to go, the NASCAR circus arrived at Rockingham, North Carolina, where Earnhardt kept the pressure on. While Ward Burton scored his first Winston Cup victory, Earnhardt, having at one time challenged for the lead, settled for 7th place. Jeff fought car setup problems and finished 20th. His lead had diminished to 162 points with just two races to go.

The penultimate race was held at Phoenix International Raceway in Arizona. Ricky Rudd crossed the finish line first, continuing a streak of 13 years in which he won at least one race. Earnhardt ran a blistering pace to finish third. But Gordon saved most of his points lead with a strong fifth-place finish, holding an advantage of 147 points over Earnhardt, the greatest driver of the era. With only one race to go, Gordon needed to finish only 41st or to lead a lap to secure the championship. The stage was set for a final showdown between the seven-time champion and the upstart kid whose star was rising fast.

The season finale was held in Hampton, Georgia, in the heart of stock-car country. Fans came in droves to watch the race that would decide the championship. They lined the fences in frenzied anticipation of the duel between Gordon and Earnhardt, the two hottest drivers of the year. Gordon's season-long dominance gave him the edge, but Earnhardt wasn't quite ready to concede the crown. He drove like the hard-nosed champion that he was, throwing his car into the corners, at the ragged edge of control, barely holding his racing line through the turn and sliding his car onto the straightaways lap after lap. It was racing genius.

Champion

Earnhardt led 268 of the race's 328 laps, taking the checkered flag at well over 150 mph. But by then, Gordon had already secured the championship. Despite

Gordon and Dale "The Intimidator" Earnhardt speak before practice for the 2001 Daytona 500. Earnhardt, NASCAR's most popular driver, was fatally injured in a crash on the race's final lap.

fighting an ill-handling car, he managed to lead the race for a lap, guaranteeing him the points for the championship. Earnhardt dominated the race, but Gordon made the smartest move.

It was during a green-flag pit stop that his crew chief radioed him and told him to come into the pit. But just as Gordon was about to pull into the pit lane, he made a split-second decision to forgo the pit stop and stay out on the track. As he was about to pull into the pit, he checked his mirrors and saw no one close enough to pass him. Aware that he would run unchallenged for a lap and that a lap led was a championship won, he made the right decision. While the other cars refueled and got fresh rubber, Jeff circled the track alone and took the lead. He finished the race in 32nd place, a lowly 14 laps behind Earnhardt, yet he was the new champion.

In just his third year in the Winston Cup Series, Gordon had accomplished his ultimate goal. Ever the team player, he credited his crew with the championship. Not only was this a career moment for Gordon, it was also a significant moment in the history of the sport. NASCAR's popularity was growing by leaps and bounds, thanks to the thrilling spectacle of fast cars and the warriors who drove them. And now, the strongest and fiercest of them all, Dale Earnhardt, had handed the reins to the next generation of winners, led by Jeff Gordon.

It's Tough at the Top

As champion, Gordon was thrust into the limelight, making public appearances all over the country. He signed on to endorse a host of products, placing him among star athletes from more traditionally popular sports such as baseball and basketball. Gordon also made television appearances, including an interview on the popular talk show *Late Night with David Letterman*. He was no longer just an up-and-coming stock-car driver—he was the new face of NASCAR.

In the follow-up to his championship season, Gordon found the going tough. He had become a driver other drivers feared. Everyone was out to beat him at all costs. That year, he battled his teammate Terry Labonte, who by mid-season held a commanding points lead. Gordon bore down like a true champion, but with four races left, the momentum swung back to Labonte's favor. The final race would determine the champion. Gordon trailed Labonte by a scant 47 points. But luck was not on his side that year, and he suffered a mechanical problem in the race that left him two laps down on the leader. Labonte finished fifth and earned his second Winston Cup championship, topping Gordon by 37 points.

Smashing Records

Gordon was determined to take back the championship in 1997. Gordon, Dale Jarrett, and Mark Martin were engaged in the closest three-way championship battle in NASCAR history. Each man had a chance to lock up the championship at the season finale at Atlanta. But when the smoke cleared, it was Gordon who stood at the top of the podium. In winning his second Winston Cup title in three years, Gordon had proven that his first championship hadn't been a fluke. His consistent driving and his team's steady approach to each race weekend became the hallmarks of Gordon and his crew.

If race fans were thrilled with the run to the 1997 championship, they must have been bored to tears with the 1998 season. But it wasn't for lack of spectacle. They were witness to one of the most dominant season-long performances in the entire history of stock-car racing. That year marked the 50th anniversary of NASCAR and featured a remarkable performance from one driver in particular. That driver was two-time champ Jeff Gordon.

Gordon takes the checkered flag in a hard fought 1997 Daytona 500. Terry Labonte, in the Kellogg's Chevrolet, and Ricky Craven follow.

Gordon and his crew would win a stunning 13 races, tying NASCAR legend Richard Petty's record. That season, it was as if he was expected to win at each track. In fact, some fans began to wear T-shirts that read, "Anyone but Gordon." His performance was simply spectacular. He won four straight in the summer, tying another modern record. His 364-point margin over Mark Martin in the final standings was the second-biggest gap of the decade. He won not one, but two $1 million bonuses in the Winston No Bull 5 program. He won the Pepsi Southern 500 for the fourth straight season, extending his own

The Pit Crew

When a driver pulls off the track and into his pit area, his pit crew is waiting for him at the ready. The crew might refuel the car, change the tires, make adjustments to the suspension, and repair any damage that may have occurred during an accident. Crews are always looking for ways to shave off a second from the time it takes to do their tasks. Each crew member has a specific job and practices it to precision.

Jeff's pit crew saw several members leave following the 1999 season, and in 2005, longtime crew chief Robbie Loomis was replaced by Steve Letarte, who began his career as a mechanic at age 18 and worked his way to the top of his profession. Mark Thoreson is the team manager. Over the past few years, the crew has brought in several new members in an attempt to regain the championship.

The pit crews at Hendrick Motorsports work out at an on-site facility with special coaches whose training programs are designed to maximize hand-eye coordination and foot speed. Jeff's pit crew also completes about eight full pit stop drills three days a week. The crew can pull a four-tire-change pit stop in 13 seconds on average.

Gordon shakes hands with stock-car legend Richard Petty during the Primestar 500 at Atlanta Motor Speedway. The seven-time champion amassed 200 victories during his career.

all-time record for wins at NASCAR's oldest superspeedway. He also won the Budweiser Pole four times.

Even more uncanny was his and his team's never-say-die approach week in and week out. A perfect example is the season finale. Even though he had sewn up the championship at the second-to-last race, the ACDelco 400, he came into the last race with a burning hunger to win. It may have been his only chance to tie one of the most cherished records in NASCAR—Richard Petty's 13 wins in a single season—and he wasn't about to let it pass him by. Gordon won the race easily and capped a historic championship season by tying Petty's mark. Gordon had truly cemented his place in the history of NASCAR as one of its all-time greats.

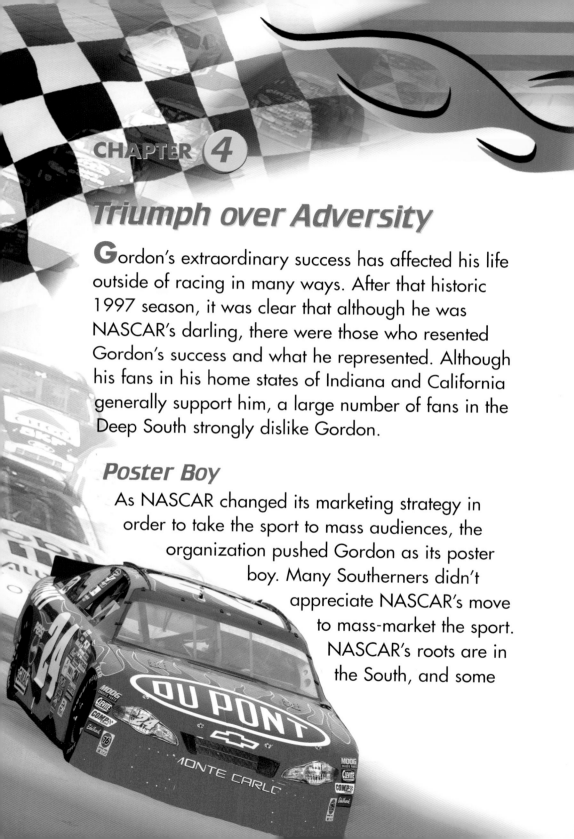

CHAPTER 4

Triumph over Adversity

Gordon's extraordinary success has affected his life outside of racing in many ways. After that historic 1997 season, it was clear that although he was NASCAR's darling, there were those who resented Gordon's success and what he represented. Although his fans in his home states of Indiana and California generally support him, a large number of fans in the Deep South strongly dislike Gordon.

Poster Boy

As NASCAR changed its marketing strategy in order to take the sport to mass audiences, the organization pushed Gordon as its poster boy. Many Southerners didn't appreciate NASCAR's move to mass-market the sport. NASCAR's roots are in the South, and some

Gordon's career took off as the popularity of NASCAR grew to an all-time high. Here he poses after the unveiling of a Tag Heuer billboard in New York's Times Square.

fans didn't like the fact that NASCAR wasn't promoting a Southern driver. As NASCAR gained more and more corporate sponsorship, these fans associated Gordon with the move from grassroots racing to corporate spectacle. This resentment was hard for Gordon to take. All he

At the 2002 Daytona 500, after crashing out of the lead on lap 195,
Gordon made a pit stop too early and was sent to the back of the field.

wanted to do was drive cars, win championships, and entertain the sport's fans.

Ignoring his detractors, Gordon continued to focus on racing. In 1999, he signed a lifetime contract with Hendrick Motorsports, giving him partial ownership of the team. He won a fourth championship in 2001, but his personal life soon took a dramatic turn for the worse. In 2002, Brooke filed for divorce. As a condition of the divorce, she sought a large share of Gordon's career earnings, which were estimated at close to $50 million, not counting endorsements. The divorce proceedings were bitter and acrimonious, and played out in the public via supermarket tabloids and more respectable media outlets as well. Gordon maintained that he loved Brooke and wished to continue to be friends with her. This drawn-out court battle took its toll on his results on the track. Gordon's winless streak had reached 31 races, the longest period without a win since his rookie season.

Comeback

Finally, in 2002, he broke the streak by scoring a win at Bristol, and then winning the following race at Darlington. That year, he won three races and finished fourth in the championship. Not bad for a driver in a slump, yet it was not good enough for Gordon or for his fans. Observers noted that he must have been distracted by the events of his life outside of racing. The divorce

forced Gordon to come to terms with who he was, the image he projected, and what he wanted out of life. "People say, 'He thinks he's Mr. Perfect,'" he told a reporter for the *St. Petersburg Times.* "There may have been times along the way I did try to live up to that and put too much pressure on myself. I'm still trying to hold a certain standard, but I'm not putting so much pressure on

36

As the field rounds the corner during the 2005 Dickies 500 at Texas Motor Speedway, Jeff Gordon runs up front alongside Matt Kenseth. Gordon qualified second fastest and finished 14th.

myself to be perfect because I know it's not possible. I've had lots of distractions for many years," he added, referring to important business decisions. "I've still been able to get in that race car and do my job, and I feel I do a good job at it. This one may be at a different level."

Gordon and the entire Hendrick Motorsports Team celebrate a victory in the winner's circle after winning the 2005 Daytona 500.

After the divorce was finalized, Gordon appeared to be more thoughtful and introspective about life's larger issues. "I think about image a lot," he told the reporter. "One of the things I'm recognizing more recently is that I'm also human, and there's nothing wrong with that. In some ways, I've earned a little bit more respect because people have recognized that I am human."

Despite his setbacks, he has been able to use his racing success to help others less fortunate than him. He created the Jeff Gordon Foundation to help children with chronic disabilities and their families. The foundation was established in 1999 and supports four charities. It also offers support on a case-by-case basis for other charitable organizations.

Triumph

As Gordon has grown, so have his business interests. In addition to his many sponsors, he is active in his own ventures, including Jeff Gordon Chevrolet, a car dealership. He also endorses a line of wines. However, none of his interests distract him from his mission: to win races. In 2003, he finished fourth in the series, and in 2005, he improved to third. In February 2005, he won his third Daytona 500, becoming the fifth driver to win three Daytona 500s and the seventh driver to win 70 NASCAR races.

Gordon had high hopes for the season, but his results were inconsistent. In September, near the end of the season, his crew chief, Robbie Loomis, resigned from the team. Loomis stayed on with Hendrick Motorsports as a consultant for driver Jimmie Johnson's team. Despite his reassignment, Loomis spoke highly of Gordon, as is reflected in the article "Still the Man to Beat," written by Thomas Pope for the Web site www.stockcarracing.com: "We all know what a winner is and he's the one all along who kept us calm. A lot of drivers have asked me what the difference is between Jeff Gordon and other drivers. I think that having won four championships, Jeff has confidence that runs way deep."

Steve Letarte, who was Gordon's car chief, took over

as crew chief. Despite inconsistent results, Gordon won the Subway 500 at Martinsville Speedway, his first victory in 22 races.

As Gordon and his fans look forward to a return to his dominant form, they can look back at a career of astounding achievements. But not all can be quantified in statistics. One of Gordon's greatest achievements has been his effect on the sport of stock-car racing as it began a transformation from local to mass-market appeal. As driver Jeff Burton said during an ESPN interview, "Jeff has been one of those people who changed what a race car driver is. Look at Richard Petty. Look at Dale Earnhardt. Look at Cale Yarborough. Then look at Jeff Gordon. That's not the same picture. Jeff helped bring mainstream young America into our sport."

With Gordon's new role as team owner, his responsibilities are gradually changing. "I'm at the shop more now because I'm a bigger part of the organization than I used to be," he noted in "Still the Man to Beat." "I have more of a say in things now and a hand in what's going on. But to be honest, my role really hasn't changed all that much. I love being involved in the ownership side of things. When I want to step away from driving, that's when my role around here will change significantly."

Gordon has many more years of driving left, so long as the motivation is there. And with the new crop of racers stepping up to the big time, there is plenty of motivation.

Gordon takes the fast way around, holding the #24 car in the groove at the 2006 Subway Fresh 500 at Phoenix International Raceway.

"The competition is stiffer now than ever before," said team founder Rick Hendrick in "Still the Man to Beat," the article on Stockcarracing.com. "But if we can control the failures and finish every race, we can leave the rest up to Jeff Gordon."

Awards

1990 United States Auto Club midgets
  championship
1991 Rookie of the Year, Busch Series
1993 Maxx Race Cards Rookie of the Year
  Winston Cup Champion
1995 Winston Cup Champion
1996 Premier 1996 Indiana Professional
  Athlete
1997 Winston Cup Champion
1997 Winner, Daytona 500
1998 Winston Cup Champion
1999 Winner, Daytona 500
2001 Winston Cup Champion
2005 Winner, Daytona 500

Glossary

apron The flat lower edge of a racetrack.

BMX A form of bicycle racing where riders compete on a dirt course with tight corners and jumps.

caution flag The flag used to signal drivers to slow down and maintain their running order.

draft When a driver positions his or her car directly behind another car in its slipstream. As the lead car works harder to cut through the wind resistance, the car drafting it can use less power to travel the same speed.

groove The line all the way around the track where the most cars have driven, making it the fastest way around the track. Loose rubber from wearing tires is crushed into the track surface, improving traction.

midget race cars Race cars powered by small engines that feature sophisticated suspension, generally raced by kids 8 to 15 years old.

perennial Lasting or active for a year or for several years.

pit A space on pit row where a car goes for service and repair during a race.

pit stop Any part of the race when a driver pulls his or her car into the pit for service.

pole position The inside position on the first row, which is the best starting position.

pundit Someone with special knowledge who expresses his or her opinion.

qualifying race A run of one or more timed laps occurring prior to the race itself. The fastest car earns pole position. Cars are given positions on the starting grid based on their qualifying times.

slipstream The area of reduced pressure or forward suction behind a fast-moving car.

speedway A racetrack of at least one mile (1.6 km) in distance.

For More Information

Daytona International Speedway
1801 W. International Speedway Boulevard
Daytona Beach, FL 32114
Web site: http://www.daytonainternationalspeedway.com

Joe Weatherly Stock Car Museum and NMPA Hall of Fame
Darlington Raceway
P.O. Box 500
Darlington, SC 29540-0500
Web site: http://www.darlingtonraceway.com/track%5Finfo/museum

The Jeff Gordon Foundation
P.O. Box 880
Harrisburg, NC 28075
Web site: http://www.jeffgordonfoundation.org

National Sprint Car Hall of Fame & Museum
One Sprint Capital Place
P.O. Box 542
Knoxville, IA 50138
(641) 842-6176
Web site: http://www.sprintcarhof.com

Web Sites

Due to the changing nature of Internet links, Rosen Publishing has developed an online list of Web sites related to the subject of this book. This site is updated regularly. Please use this link to access the list:

http://www.rosenlinks.com/bw/jego

For Further Reading

Buckley, James. *NASCAR* (DK Eyewitness Books). New York, NY: DK Children, 2005.

Gordon, Jeff. *Jeff Gordon: Portrait of a Champion*. New York, NY: Perennial Currents, 1998.

Grist, Jeff, and Memo Gidley. *Karting: Everything You Need to Know*. St. Paul, MN: Motorbooks International, 2006.

NASCAR Scene Editors. *Thunder and Glory: The 25 Most Memorable Races in NASCAR Winston Cup History*. Chicago, IL: Triumph Books, 2006.

Savage, Jeff. *Jeff Gordon* (Amazing Athletes). Minneapolis, MN: LernerSports, 2003.

Stewart, Mark. *Auto Racing: A History of Fast Cars and Fearless Drivers*. New York, NY: Franklin Watts, 1998.

White, Ben, and Nigel Kinrade. *NASCAR Racers: Today's Top Drivers*, 2006 Edition. Sarasota, FL: Crestline, 2006.

Woods, Bob. *Pit Pass: Behind the Scenes of NASCAR* (NASCAR Middle Grade Book). Pleasantville, NY: Reader's Digest Children's Books, 2005.

Bibliography

Brinster, Richard. *Jeff Gordon*. Philadelphia, PA: Chelsea House Publishers, 1997.

The Jeff Gordon Network. Retrieved April 2, 2006 (http://www. jeffgordon.com/home/default.sps?itype=12215).

Jeff Gordon Online. "The Bickford Effect." 2004. Retrieved April 5, 2006 (http://www.gordonline.com/editorials/050204.html).

McGuire, Ann. *The History of NASCAR*. Philadelphia, PA: Chelsea House Publishers, 1997.

Owens, Thomas S., and Diana Star Helmer. *NASCAR*. Brookfield, CT: Twenty-First Century Books, 2000.

Pope, Thomas. "Still the Man to Beat." *Stock Car Racing*. Retrieved April 31, 2006 (http://www.stockcarracing.com/thehistoryof/ bio/134_0304_feat).

Puma, Mike. "Gordon, a Boy and His Car." ESPN.com. Retrieved April 4, 2006 (http://espn.go.com/classic/biography/s/ Gordon_Jeff.html).

Index

About the Author

J. Poolos is the author of seven other Rosen books, including one on freestyle motocross jumper and motocross racer Travis Pastrana. In his spare time he rides motorcycles and reads everything he can about racing.

Photo Credits

Cover © Jon Ferrey/Getty Images; p. 1 © Chris Stanford/Getty Images; pp. 5, 6, 7, 38 © Streeter Lecka/Getty Images; p. 14 © Rusty Jarrett/Getty Images; pp. 17, 19 © Focus on Sport/Getty Images; pp. 20, 21 © Steve Swope/Allsport; p. 24 © Jed Jacobsohn/Getty Images; p. 26 © Bob Sweeten/Associated Press, AP; p. 29 © Phil Coale/Associated Press, AP; p.31 © David Taylor/Getty Images; p. 33 © David Karp/Associated Press, AP; p. 34 © Reuters/Corbis; pp. 36, 37 © Harold Hinson/TSN/ZUMA/Corbis; p.41 © Icon SMI/Corbis.

Designer: Gene Mollica